MARVEL
IRON MAN 3™
THE MOVIE STORYBOOK

ADAPTED BY MICHAEL GIGLAIN

BASED ON A SCREENPLAY BY DREW PEARCE & SHANE BLACK

PRODUCED BY KEVIN FEIGE

DIRECTED BY SHANE BLACK

Printed in the United States of America

First Edition

1 3 5 7 9 10 8 6 4 2

G942-9090-6-13032

ISBN 978-1-4231-7251-2

TM & © 2013 MARVEL & SUBS.
marvelkids.com

MARVEL

NEW YORK

SUSTAINABLE FORESTRY INITIATIVE

Certified Sourcing
www.sfiprogram.org
SFI-00993
For Text Only

TONY STARK WAS HAVING A BAD DAY.

Yes, Tony was a brilliant scientist and a billionaire inventor, and everyone knew him to be the Super Hero Iron Man. And yes, it was the holiday season, and everyone was supposed to be spreading good cheer. But Tony Stark was still having a bad day.

Tony was unable to move. The Mark XLII was leaking black oil onto the white snow as Tony looked up into the starry sky and thought about what had just happened. He remembered the surprise attack on his mansion and the spectacular explosions. He also remembered jumping into his Iron Man armor and coming to the rescue. But his armor was damaged during the battle, and with his power supply dangerously low, the Armored Avenger had crashed into the snowy fields of rural Tennessee.

But that's not where this story starts, Tony thought as he slowly lifted his head from the snow-covered field. Tony remembered the woman who appeared at his home just before the sneak attack. Her name was Maya Hansen, and she was a scientist also. Tony had first seen her on New Year's Eve, 1999, with his bodyguard and driver, Happy Hogan. They were in Bern, Switzerland, and it was almost midnight . . .

Tony had just given a speech at the Bern Tech Conference when he met Maya Hansen. She was a beautiful research scientist who was interested in Tony's genius intellect, but Tony was just interested in meeting Maya because she was pretty. Then Tony heard about her scientific theories and had to learn more about them.

AS TONY, MAYA, AND HAPPY WERE LEAVING the conference hall, they were stopped by a skinny man with a cane named Aldrich Killian. Killian was putting together a team of scientists for his new organization called Advanced Idea Mechanics, or A.I.M for short, and he wanted Maya and Tony to join him.

Tony quickly escorted Killian away and began to study Maya's notes. She was very smart, but Tony was smarter, and with a little quick thinking, Tony adjusted Maya's formula so that her scientific theory would work! Soon, the clock counted down to midnight, and there was a big celebration. After the party ended, everyone went their separate ways.

But that still doesn't explain how Iron Man crash-landed in the middle of Tennessee, Tony thought as he began to lug his very heavy Iron Man armor through the deep snow. Then he thought back to just a few days ago, when he was in the Middle East with the U.S. Army.

THE INVINCIBLE IRON MAN WAS ON A MISSION TO LOCATE AND DESTROY LAND MINES that had been made by Stark Industries.

Just as he finished clearing the mines, Iron Man heard an explosion in the distance and rocketed off to help. He landed to find American troops in the middle of a firefight. They had been outnumbered until Iron Man arrived!

With a few quick shots of his Repulsor beams, Iron Man quickly destroyed the enemy's weapons and led the American troops into a secret underground bunker.

The inside of the bunker looked like a movie theater, complete with a very large screen, comfy chairs, and buckets of popcorn. Iron Man looked at the soldiers, and they looked back to him. This is not what they expected to find inside the safe house in the middle of the desert. Then one soldier saw a remote control and carefully pressed PLAY.

The screen came to life with the image of a hooded figure who introduced himself only as the Mandarin. Iron Man listened intently as the madman threatened the United States. Iron Man knew that he had to stop the Mandarin, but he also knew that doing so wouldn't be easy. Iron Man needed help, and he knew the perfect man for the job—his best friend, Colonel James Rhodes, who also happened to be the armored hero known as War Machine!

Outside of a restaurant in Malibu, California, sat a row of motorcycles . . . and two armored suits.

One belonged to Tony and the other belonged to Rhodey—but something was different about his. Instead of the familiar gray and black plated armor, it was now red, white, and blue.

Inside, Rhodey told Tony about how War Machine had changed into Iron Patriot. Tony teased his old friend, and that's when Rhodey knew that there was something else going on with Tony, something big.

Tony was telling Rhodey that people wanted the Super Hero, not the man, when suddenly, Tony's chest felt tight.

He couldn't breathe and was gasping for air. He fell to the ground as Rhodey and the other people in the restaurant looked on in shock. Tony crawled outside and into his Iron Man armor, where he knew he'd be safe.

Suddenly, there was a knock on Tony's helmet.

"You okay in there?" Rhodey asked.

"Never better. Gotta go." And with that, Iron Man fired his boosters and launched into the sky. Rhodey looked on with worry.

INSIDE STARK INDUSTRIES the beautiful Virginia "Pepper" Potts—CEO of Stark Industries and also Tony's longtime girlfriend—sat opposite her new head of security, Happy Hogan, who was Tony's former driver and bodyguard. Pepper had a big meeting with Aldrich Killian to discuss his Extremis Project. Happy recognized Killian's name and was surprised to see a handsome, muscular man walk into the room with no cane.

Happy watched from outside the conference room as Killian was presenting his idea to Pepper, which involved "upgrading" the human brain. But then Happy had seen a suspicious figure lurking about the hallways and followed him outside. The man was sitting on Pepper's car, and that bothered Happy. After confronting the man, Happy learned that his name was Savin and that he was working with Killian and A.I.M.

Just then, Pepper and Killian walked up. Killian was still trying to convince Pepper to join his team and help fund the Extremis Project, but Pepper was not interested. As Killian and Savin drove away, Happy got a bad feeling in the pit of his stomach. This will not end well, he thought.

Back at his mansion, Tony was hard at work on his latest armor: the Mark XLII. Controlled by his mind, the Mark XLII could fly to Tony from across great distances, just by thought. That is, if it worked.

Tony was still figuring out all of the little details when Pepper interrupted him. She told him that the Mandarin had attacked once more, and that survivors of this attack had been taken to a nearby hospital.

When Pepper turned around, she was standing face-to-face with Tony, who was already in his Iron Man Mark XLII armor and ready for action.

"Don't wait up," Tony said as he flew off into the night!

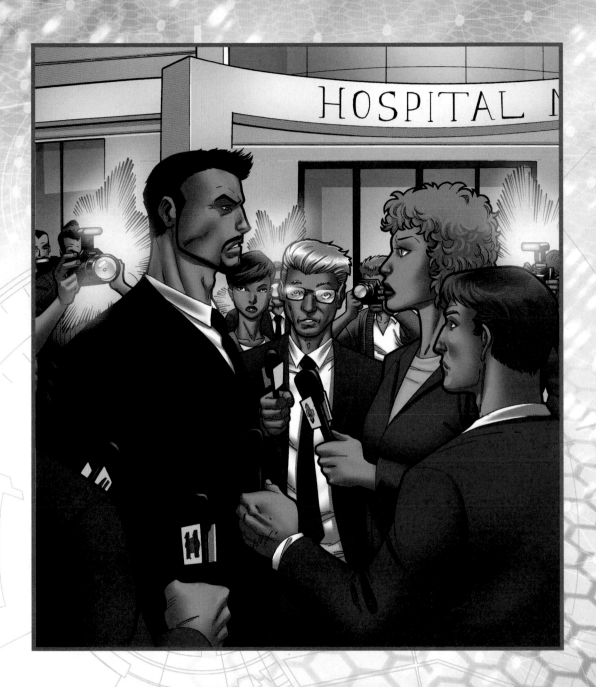

As Iron Man flew toward the hospital, he thought about keeping the people closest to him safe. When he landed, he ejected out of his suit so as not to cause a scene. But a scene was already unfolding: reporters curious about the Mandarin's latest attack.

Tony looked directly into the news camera. "Enough games," he began. "You want a fight, here's my address." Tony was challenging the Mandarin to stop hiding and fight Iron Man one-on-one. It was the Mandarin's move.

The next night, the Mandarin responded with another taped message. This time, the Mandarin was in a dark and decrepit lair. He reached out to a large pile of fortune cookies. "Here's one..." the Mandarin began as he removed the paper inside the fragile cookie. "'You will absolutely destroy Iron Man today,'" the villain read with an evil smile. "Woah, that's specific."

Tony, watching the performance from his home, instructed JARVIS to look for traces of a bomb. There had been an explosion during the Mandarin's last attack, but no sign of a bomb, and this intrigued Tony, but his thoughts were interrupted when the doorbell rang.

Pepper answered the door to find a beautiful woman asking to see Tony. When Tony got there, he recognized the woman as scientist Maya Hansen. As the three of them began to talk, Maya noticed something odd on the television. The footage showed Tony's mansion, and it had a small dot moving faster and faster toward it. When Tony turned to look, he realized what the dot was: an incoming missile!

They were under attack!

THE POWERFUL MISSILE RACED ACROSS THE CALIFORNIA SKY

searching for its target: Tony Stark's mansion. Its time to detonation: now!

KA-THOOM! Tony was thrown across the room as huge explosions rocked his house. Pieces of glass and large chunks of metal debris went flying in every direction. Immediately, Tony yelled to JARVIS and ordered the Mark XLII armor to fly to Pepper and wrap around her. If Pepper were safe, then she could also rescue Maya. Tony would just have to find another way out!

More explosions shook the building as Pepper looked through the Iron Man helmet. She had never been inside the suit before and was amazed at how things looked through Iron Man's eyes. But Pepper had little time to enjoy the suit or familiarize herself with it because more missiles were headed her way.

Tony yelled at Pepper to save Maya and then get as far away from the mansion as possible. But he, too, needed saving as he ducked from flying debris of concrete, glass, and shrapnel.

Obeying to Tony, Pepper lifted her arm and fired a Repulsor beam at the wall. The impact from the blast knocked her back a bit, but when the smoke cleared, there was a huge hole where the living room wall used to be.

Pepper grabbed Maya, quickly fired the suit's boosters, and flew awkwardly out of the mansion just before more missiles hit.

Just as Pepper and Maya landed safely away from the crumbling house, the Iron Man armor opened, releasing Pepper from her metal shell. The Mark XLII then rocketed back toward the destruction to find Tony.

Tony leaped inside the armor as soon as it arrived, though it was badly damaged from all the explosions. He commanded the suit to fire its missiles, but they merely dropped to the ground. His targeting system was also damaged! Thinking quickly, Tony picked up the missiles and hurled them at the helicopters. He then shot a Repulsor blast at his own missiles, causing them to explode and take down the Mandarin's choppers!

When more heavily armored helicopters appeared outside his window, Tony fired his Repulsor blasts at his expensive Baby Grand piano. The force of the beams pushed the piano through the giant hole in the wall and onto the blades of the copter, causing it crashing into the water below.

But with more attack helicopters and missiles heading his way, Tony knew he was outnumbered. He couldn't let the Mandarin get his hands on his Iron Man armor or inventions, so Tony did the only thing he could think of: he instructed JARVIS to blow up all seven original Iron Man armors—the Marks I to VII—so that they would not fall into the clutches of the Mandarin.

As the choppers attacked and the suits exploded, the mansion sank into the ocean—and so did Iron Man! Using all of the suit's emergency power, Tony flew out of the water unnoticed by the helicopters.

He flew away as far and as fast as he could, but his suit was so damaged and so low on energy that he could not keep it in the air. Iron Man crashed into a snowy field in the middle of Tennessee.

Tony slowly ejected himself from the armor and dragged it through the snow to a lone phone booth on the side of the road. He needed to check on Pepper…and tell her that he was still alive.

After leaving Pepper a message, Tony spotted an old shed and hoped that it would contain the tools that he would need to fix his armor. He dragged the suit to the shed and kicked the door in, gradually lifting the armor onto a workbench. With JARVIS powered down, Tony was all alone.

Or so he thought.

Tony heard something behind him and turned around to see a young boy staring at him. "No way!" the boy yelled. "Iron Man is here!"

Tony thought the boy was talking about him, but Harley corrected him. "No, you're Tony Stark!" the boy said. "You're boring!"

Tony Stark gave a wry smile. He looked around at Harley's science trophies above the workbench and guessed that he had been bullied at school. Tony then pulled a silver capsule from the armor and gave it to Harley to use against bullies in exchange for his help. This was the beginning of a beautiful friendship.

They would need supplies to rebuild the armor, so they head into town.

Wearing borrowed clothes, Tony and Harley walked down Main Street in Rose Hill, Tennessee, in search of the necessary materials to fix the armor. But something wasn't right. A car was slowly driving behind them, and Tony had the feeling that they were being watched.

Inside the car were Brandt and Savin, two agents of the Mandarin and A.I.M.

Tony turned to see two people charging toward them, but they didn't look like regular people. Savin was glowing with energy, and Brandt's hands were radiating heat. Using their enhanced abilities, they attacked Tony and Harley!

Yelling to Harley, Tony told him to use that silver capsule he gave him earlier. Harley did as instructed and threw the capsule at Savin. The capsule exploded, temporarily blinding Savin and allowing Harley to escape.

Meanwhile, Brandt had Tony cornered. But just as she was about to attack, Tony pulled back his sleeve to reveal a makeshift Repulsor ray. He fired a blast at Brandt, that knocked her across the street and into the snow!

WITH BRANDT AND SAVIN MOMENTARILY DEFEATED, Tony and

Harley were able to escape. Tony said goodbye to Harley, and thanked him for all of his help. Tony then jumped into Brandt and Savin's car and drove away.

While driving through a nearby town, Tony noticed a parked news van. He quickly jumped into the back of the van and used its computers to get information on the Mandarin.

Tony's research pointed him to A.I.M. and Aldrich Killian, who were working on enhancing human DNA with their Extremis Project. That's when Tony realized why there was no bomb during the Mandarin's first attack: one of the *people* must have been the bomb!

Just like with Brandt and Savin, one of the Mandarin's men must have had super powers, including the ability to explode. Tony realized that the Mandarin must be working with A.I.M.

Tony had to find them, and fast!

With JARVIS slowly coming back online, Tony was able to pinpoint the Mandarin's videotape transmissions to Miami, Florida, and he immediately headed for the Sunshine State.

TONY snuck into the Mandarin's mansion. Unfortunately, as he was about to confront the villain, He was knocked out from behind!

He woke to find himself in a cell—with Rhodey! Out of the shadows stepped Killian and Maya. From them, Tony learned the Mandarin had the Iron Patriot armor and that Killian and Maya were working for the villain! Killian cackled in delight, but Tony had a plan.

Just then, the wall of Tony's cell exploded as an iron gauntlet and metal boot from the Mark XLII suit crashed through the wall. Tony had called the armor with his mind, but not all of it had arrived at the same time.

The Mandarin's men wasted no time in attacking. And Tony would have to fight back with just a boot and a glove.

Back in Tennessee, Harley heard rattling coming from the shed. He slowly opened the door. The rest of the Mark XLII burst out and streaked into the sky! The armor was on it's way to find its target—Tony Stark!

CLINK . . . CLINK . . . . CLINK . . . CLANK! CLANK! CLANK!

"'BOUT TIME, BOYS!" Tony said as the remainder of his armor had finally arrived. Iron Man was now ready for action, and quickly took out the rest of the Mandarin's men with Repulsor beams and iron punches. When he turned to look for Killian, the menace of A.I.M. was gone, and so was Maya Hansen.

So many questions were racing through Tony's brain. How could this have happened? Why is Killian working with the Mandarin? And what about Maya? What role did she play in all of this? Tony sighed. He had been betrayed by an old friend. Tony had to find them and get answers. But he wouldn't have time to look for them now because the Mandarin had taken Pepper hostage! Things were not looking good for Iron Man . . .

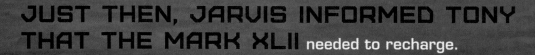

JUST THEN, JARVIS INFORMED TONY THAT THE MARK XLII needed to recharge.

And Tony and Rhodey had yet another problem on their hands: Savin was wearing the Iron Patriot armor and was heading toward Air Force One—for the President of the United States!

As they jumped in a speedboat, Tony made some adjustments to the suit as Rhodey raced to stop Savin!

With the Iron Man armor at 92% power, it rocketed into the sky toward Air Force One to save the President from the Mandarin's men. Iron Patriot had broken into the President's cabin and revealed himself to be working for the Mandarin. Just as Savin was about to fire a Repulsor beam, there was a huge THUD! as something rocked the plane.

STANDING BEHIND SAVIN WAS THE INVINCIBLE IRON MAN!

The two armored suits exchanged iron blows and Repulsor blasts, one of which ripped a huge hole on the side of Air Force One!

Iron Man looked out the window and was shocked to see people falling from the side of the plane!

IRON MAN UNLEASHED A MIGHTY REPULSOR BLAST, knocking the Iron Patriot back against the inside of the plane. Then Tony rocketed out of the hole and down to the falling people. Thinking fast, he quickly locked arms with one of them.

He dove down, and the passenger he had locked arms with then locked his arm with the next person falling. This continued with with each falling passenger all the way down, resulting in a strange, midair monkey ladder.

During the commotion aboard Air Force One, Savin trapped the President with him inside the Iron Patriot suit and rocketed out of the plane with him. He had kidnapped President Ellis!

With the President in his grasp, the Mandarin released another video message.

The villain was holding the President high above an oil tanker. The Mandarin's plan was to ignite the oil onboard, causing a giant explosion and contaminating the waters of the Gulf Coast.

And to make matters worse, the bomb was going to go off on December 25th—Christmas Day!

Tony was again armor-less. He knew that they would have to rescue the President, save Pepper, and stop Killian and the Mandarin . . . alone.

And that's when he spotted Rhodey on the docks! Together they devised a plan to distract the Extremis gaurds nearby. But just as they put their plan into action, Tony heard a familiar humming sound and smiled.

All of Tony's Iron Man suits had come to save the day! There was

HEARTBREAKER, RED SNAPPER, SILVER CENTURION, BONES, SHOTGUN, AND HAMMERHEAD! EVEN NIGHTCLUB, GEMINI, AND THE BEHEMOTH IGOR HAD COME FOR A FIGHT!

Wasting no time, the Iron Men quickly attacked, firing Repulsor beams and missiles at all of the super-powered Extremis guards. Explosions rang out as armors were destroyed and Extremis guards were defeated. Meanwhile, Rhodey ran off to rescue the President and reclaim the Iron Patriot armor while Tony went to save Pepper from a particularly large and intimidating Extremis guard.

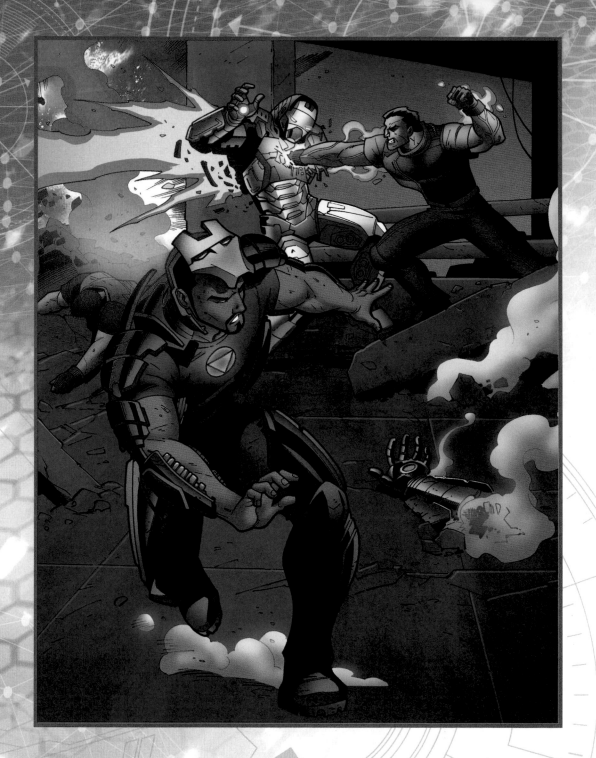

This Extremis guard was larger than the others. He lunged at Tony, and a new battle began!

But Tony had another trick up his sleeve. He called the Mark XLII armor to him, and it quickly raced across the country in formation.

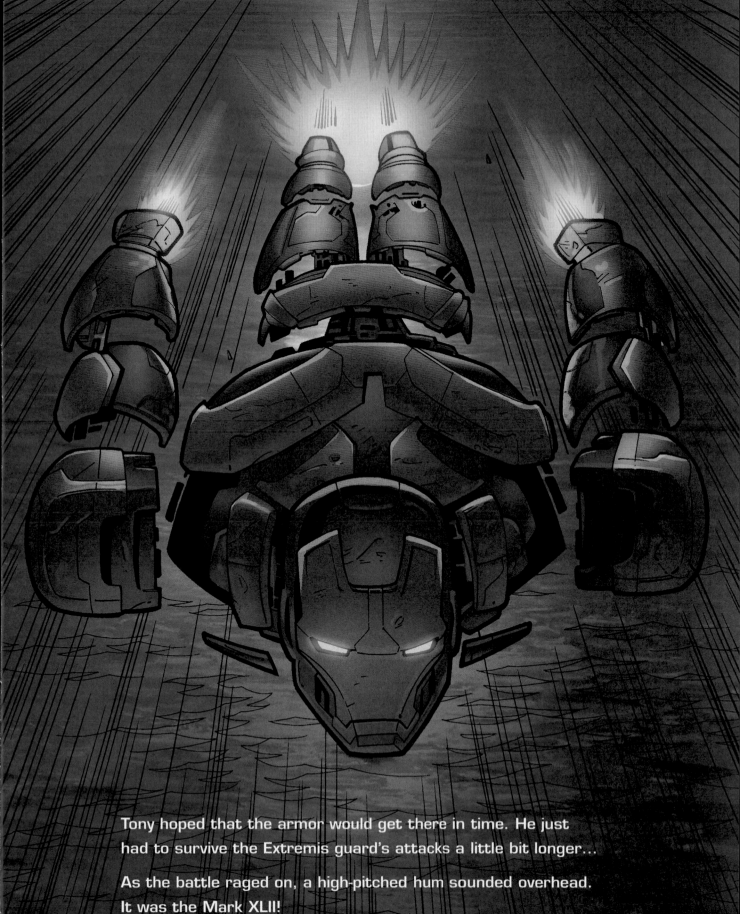

Tony hoped that the armor would get there in time. He just had to survive the Extremis guard's attacks a little bit longer...

As the battle raged on, a high-pitched hum sounded overhead. It was the Mark XLII!

From the safety of his hidden lair, the Mandarin watched in anger as his plans were destroyed before him!

Finally the Mark XLII armor arrived and Tony sprang into action. Like a matador, Tony weaved and dodged punches as he directed each piece of armor onto his opponent.

The Extremis guard laughed at Tony and his silly plan. Just then, Tony quietly whispered to JARVIS. "Blow the suit." And with that, the Mark XLII armor—with the villain still inside—erupted into a spectacular explosion!

WHEN THE SMOKE CLEARED, TONY SAW THAT THE BATTLE HAD ENDED.

The authorities had arrived, and the remaining Extremis guards had given up. The President had been saved, but both Killian and the Mandarin were still on the loose. Even still, all of the Mandarin's men were either captured or defeated and would not threaten anyone ever again.

And most of all, Pepper was safe and sound. As the two embraced, Tony realized just what—and who—was important to him.

The experiences of the last few days made Tony think about his life. He would always be Iron Man, but right now it was time for him to be Tony Stark, and one of the things that Tony Stark did best was help people— especially those in need or those who had helped him in the past—and that led him to think about someone else...

AS NEW YEAR'S EVE ROLLED AROUND,

Harley walked through the ramshackle door of his Tennessee shed to discover that the inside had been transformed into a state-of-the-art laboratory and high-tech workstation. The boy was amazed and knew exactly who was responsible for this unbelievable upgrade.

Harley smiled to himself. He now had a new favorite Super Hero, and his name was Tony Stark.